# The Carrotberry Caper

by Uma Kashnaswami • illustrated by Lydia Halverson

BEST PRACTICES IN READING
Classroom Library

# Contents

# A Cool New Crop

Mike Perry couldn't stop grinning. "We did it, Tanya! This is going to be a great project!"

Mike and Tanya had come in second place at last year's science fair. Since then, the two friends had been working on a project to win them first place this year.

"Wow!" said Tanya. "An experiment that finally worked! We've grown a plant that's half vegetable and half fruit!"

For months, Mike and Tanya had tested ways to grow veggie-fruits. They mixed pollen from the flowers of different fruits and vegetables. Their idea was to grow a food that combined the best part from each plant. Finally, one of their experimental plants had actually grown a veggie-fruit. It looked and tasted like a strawberry, but it had carrot crunch and vitamins.

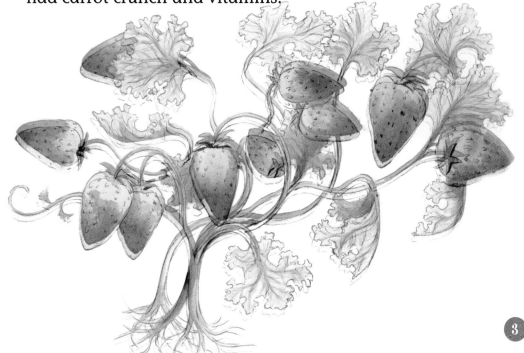

Tanya touched the rough leaves of one of the vines. Only a couple of the vines had ripe veggie-fruit on them. Mike gently plucked one off and popped it in his mouth.

"Yum," he said. "Strawberry sweetness and carrot crunch."

"What are we going to call them?" asked Tanya.

Mike scratched his head. "I don't know. Let's go to The Plant and show my dad. Maybe he'll have some ideas."

Mike dropped a few of the ripe veggie-fruits into his empty sandwich bag. Then he and Tanya set out to walk the six blocks to the college science lab. Everyone called the building "The Plant" because of the giant bean plant painted on the building.

Mike's dad was a plant scientist. He was helping Mike and Tanya with their project.

"Hi, Mrs. Mendez," said Mike as he came into the building. Mrs. Mendez flashed them a big smile from behind the front desk.

"Hi kids! I'll let your dad know you're here," she said. She listened on her telephone headset. "He wants you to wait a minute," she said. "He's got some people with him."

Tanya sniffed the air. "What's that awful smell?"

Mrs. Mendez made a face. "It's from the student lab down the hall. They're working on cauliflower. They're trying to get rid of that horrible odor when you cook it. But they seem to have turned the smell up, not down."

"No kidding," said Mike. "It smells like sweaty socks."

"I wouldn't tell your dad that," laughed Mrs. Mendez. She listened again to her headset. "Your dad says to come on in now," she said.

Mike and Tanya went down the hall to Professor Perry's lab. Suddenly, a man and a woman rushed out of the lab, almost knocking Mike down.

"Hey!" Mike cried. "Watch where you're going!"

The man stopped and looked at Professor Perry. "You'll be sorry…" the strange man muttered.

"Yes, we'll get our hands on it, one way or another," added the woman. A pin on her jacket gleamed in the hallway light. Mike saw it was shaped like a shiny, red tomato.

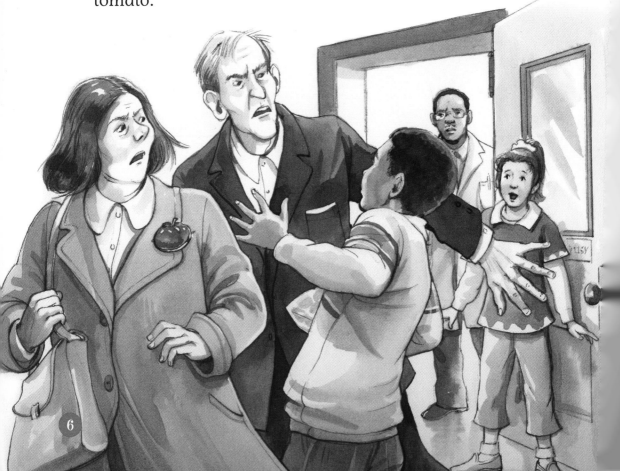

Mike's father came out of the lab. "Hi Mike. Hello, Tanya."

"Dad, is everything okay?" Mike asked. "Who were those people?"

"Nothing to worry about, son," said Professor Perry. He looked quickly up and down the hallway. "Some people just can't take 'No' for an answer. What's up with you two?"

The kids told him about their new crop of veggie-fruit. "Well, well," Mike's father said. "Do you have them with you? May I take a look?"

Mike handed the bag of veggie-fruit to his dad. "These are all the ripe ones," he said.

Professor Perry took out a veggie-fruit. He bit into it and crunched. "Nice work. Maybe you're onto something here," he said.

Mike told him they still needed to figure out a name for the veggie-fruit.

"Well, let's go celebrate your success with a picnic in the park," said Professor Perry. "We'll come up with a name while we eat." He hurried them from the lab and out the building.

As they sat at a picnic table, the three tried to think of clever names for the veggie-fruit. Carberry? Berryrot? Strawcar? They finally settled on carrotberries. Tanya said, "I like it. It has a crunchy-sweet sound."

"It's also the sound of science fair success!" added Mike.

In bed that night, Mike thought back to the two people who had rushed out of his dad's lab. They had seemed angry. Who were they and what did they want?

Dad had been excited about the carrotberries. He'd looked like he was thinking about something else during their picnic, though. Was it the mysterious visitors?

What had the man and woman said? You'll be sorry… We'll get our hands on it.

*On what?* Mike wondered, half asleep. *Oops*, he thought. *I left the carrotberries at Dad's lab. No one had better get their hands on our science fair project.*

Mike yawned. He drifted off to sleep and dreamed about the judges hanging a gold medal around his neck.

1 Why are Mike and Tanya excited about their science fair project?

2 Why would Professor Perry be able to help Mike and Tanya with their project?

3 What might the mysterious man and woman want from Professor Perry?

4 If you could cross a vegetable and a fruit, which ones would you pick? Explain your answer.

# Strange Results

The next afternoon, Tanya had trumpet practice. Mike decided to go down to The Plant after school. He wanted to get his carrotberries before someone ate them or threw them away. He needed them for the judges to taste at the science fair.

Professor Perry was in a meeting, but Mrs. Mendez let Mike into the lab. Mike saw that the carrotberries were still in the sandwich bag on the counter.

"Thanks, Mrs. Mendez," he said, picking up the bag. It felt sticky.

"Did you find what you were looking for?" she asked.

"Uh…yes. Thanks." Mike took a quick look in the bag. The carrotberries were coated with some kind of purple, gooey liquid. They looked all right, though, so he decided not to worry about it.

Mike and Tanya planned to put the finishing touches on their project over the weekend. The science fair was in just two days. Tanya arrived at Mike's house right after breakfast.

"Come on by The Plant after lunch," said Mike's father, as he left for work. "I'll take you to the campus cafe for a milkshake. Who knows? Carrotberry could be the next new flavor!"

"We'd better get started," Mike said. "We've still got to finish our taste tests. We've only got five ripe carrotberries left. Let's split one for our test."

Tanya took one of the ripe carrotberries from the bag and carefully sliced it in half. Mike rinsed the rest of the berries until the purple, gooey liquid was gone.

The carrotberries were perfect. In fact, they tasted amazingly better than the first ones they had tried! The flavor just exploded in their mouths. The carrotberries were crisp like carrots, but as juicy as the ripest strawberries.

Mike could see those science fair medals dancing in front of his eyes.

"Do you see what I see?" Tanya whispered to Mike.

"I sure do," said Mike dreamily. "That medal is going to look great hanging around my neck!"

"No, Mike," said Tanya. "Look at the wall." She pointed across the room.

Mike looked at the wall. He blinked. Then he blinked again. The wall seemed to have faded away. It was like a faint shadow he could see through. Mike could see straight into the dining room. The table had a vase of flowers on it.

"Wow," Mike said softly. "This is amazing. I sure didn't expect *this* test result."

Tanya and Mike forgot about their taste tests. They slowly turned in circles, testing their strange new abilities. They discovered they could see through all of the walls. Tanya and Mike took turns hiding in different rooms in the house, but finding each other was easy when the walls were invisible.

"Mike," Tanya said. "Do you think this works in the dark? Turn out the lights and let's see what happens."

Mike switched off the lights. They could still see perfectly.

"This is *so* cool," he grinned.

"Really, really cool," Tanya agreed.

"Come on, let's go see Dad," said Mike. He flipped the lights back on and grabbed the bag of carrotberries. He called The Plant and told Mrs. Mendez they were on their way. They had big news for Professor Perry.

On the way to The Plant, Mike and Tanya kept testing their new powers. "They're getting weaker," Tanya pointed out. It had now been almost an hour since they'd eaten the carrotberries.

"These superpowers must disappear as the carrotberries get digested," said Mike. "There's something else," Mike added.

He told Tanya about the sticky purple stuff that had appeared in the bag with the carrotberries. Had it done something to their science fair project?

**1** What is different about the second batch of carrotberries?

**2** How do Mike and Tanya test their new powers?

**3** Why is Mike now worried about their science fair project?

**4** Describe a time when something you planned didn't happen the way you expected.

# Where's Professor Perry?

When Mike and Tanya reached The Plant, Mrs. Mendez wasn't anywhere around. They decided to head straight for Professor Perry's lab. As soon as they looked through the open door, they knew something was terribly wrong.

Professor Perry's lab was a mess. Lab equipment had been knocked over. Papers were everywhere. It looked like a tornado had hit the room.

"Dad?" called Mike.

There was no answer. There was no sign of the professor, either.

"Careful," warned Tanya. "Watch your step. There's some of that purple stuff on the floor."

Mike bent down and picked something up. "Look at this."

"What is it?" asked Tanya.

"It's that woman's pin. She was wearing it when she was here that time," Mike said. He put the pin into his pocket. "Come on," he said. "We have to find Dad and those people." But how?

Tanya knocked on the door to the smelly cauliflower lab. "No, sorry, we haven't seen Professor Perry," said the young man who opened the door. "Want to try some cauliflower? It really grows on you."

"No, thanks," said Tanya. She and Mike rushed back toward the front desk.

Mrs. Mendez had returned and was looking frantic. "I'm so glad you're here," she cried. "Those strange people came back this morning. I called your dad to tell him you were coming. He didn't answer the phone so I went to the door. I heard him arguing with them. They said something about a secret formula. The next thing I knew, that man and woman had him by the arms and were shoving him out of the building!"

"Where did they go?" Tanya asked.

"I don't know," Mrs. Mendez said. "I ran out to the parking lot and saw them climb into a white van and speed off. Oh dear, I have a bad feeling about this."

"Why would they kidnap my dad and wreck his lab?" Mike asked. He was getting mad. "What could he possibly have that they…" Suddenly, Mike felt his skin grow cold. "Mrs. Mendez, do you know where my father's taste trick formula for Smith Medical is?" he asked.

"The professor locks all his important materials in his safe," said Mrs. Mendez. "I don't have the combination, so there's no way of knowing what's inside."

"Actually, I think there is," said Mike.

Mike and Tanya explained their new powers to Mrs. Mendez as they all raced back to the professor's lab. Mike and Tanya each ate a carrotberry. Soon, they were able to see into the safe. There was a bottle of purple liquid inside.

**1** How do Mike and Tanya know that something is wrong?

**2** What does Mike find that might be a clue to what happened?

**3** Why might a medical company want a taste trick formula?

**4** Where do you think Professor Perry is? Explain your answer.

# Getting a Sign

"Do you know who those people in the white van are?" Tanya asked Mrs. Mendez. "Are they with a company or something?"

"I know they gave a business name when they called for the appointment. Let me think." Mrs. Mendez closed her eyes and tried to remember. "I've got it," she said at last. "They said they were from Fowler's."

"Fowler's? What's that?" asked Tanya. "Can we look it up in the phone book?"

Mike and Tanya got out a phone book and looked under the "F's." They found three pages of Fowlers. There were only a few businesses with Fowler in the name, though. There were two dentists, a pet shop, a restaurant, and a lab equipment company.

"Lab equipment, that must be it," said Mike.

Tanya called the company's number. The woman who answered didn't know anything about a man and a woman in a white van.

Next, they called Dr. Fowler, a dentist. He must have been talking through his mask because they had no idea what he said.

"We need to think of some other way to find the professor," said Mrs. Mendez. "It's getting late and it's already dark outside. Do those carrotberries have any other superpowers that might come in handy right now?"

"Of course!" said Mike, snapping his fingers.

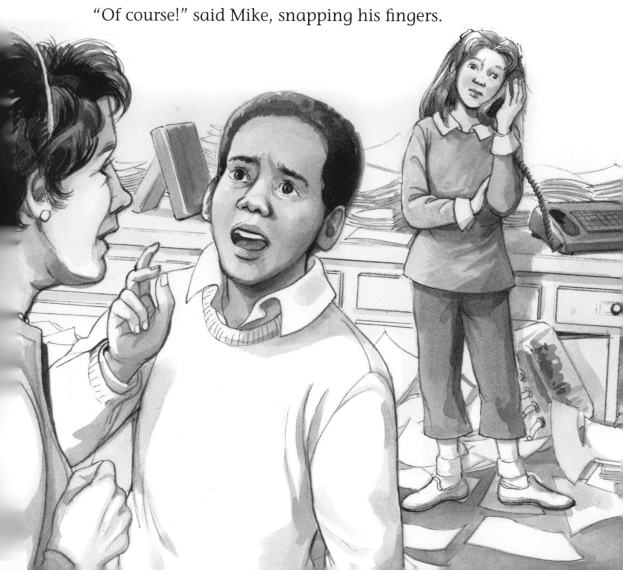

"Really?" said Mrs. Mendez excitedly. "Well, grab a handful and start chewing!"

"No, I just remembered something," said Mike. "Fowler's Kitchen. It's a new restaurant on campus."

"That's right," said Mrs. Mendez. "I think it's next to the library."

Mike nodded. "That's the one. Dad went there for a meeting once. He told Mom and me that he hated to spend good money on bad food."

"Why did he say that?" asked Tanya.

"I don't know," Mike said. "He just said that all the food tasted the same—really bad."

"Come on, then. Let's go," said Tanya.

Mike and Tanya piled into Mrs. Mendez's car. As they pulled up to Fowler's Kitchen, Mike pointed at the sign. It was shaped like a red tomato.

"Look at that," he cried. "That sign looks just like the pin that woman dropped in the lab."

"Quick! Turn your headlights off!" Tanya told Mrs. Mendez.

A white van was parked right next to the restaurant's front door.

**1** How do Mike, Tanya, and Mrs. Mendez figure out where Professor Perry might be?

**2** Why does Mrs. Mendez want Mike to eat more carrotberries?

**3** Why is the white van parked in front of the Fowler's Kitchen restaurant?

**4** What would you do if you were Mike or Tanya? Explain your answer.

# Seeing Through Walls

Mike and Tanya ate the last two carrotberries. They would need all the super help they could get.

"Those were our last ripe carrotberries," Mike said with a sigh. "But nothing's more important than saving my dad. Let's go. Be very quiet!"

Mike, Tanya, and Mrs. Mendez crept out of the car. Mike and Tanya focused their eyes on the restaurant walls. Soon, the walls seemed to fade away and they could see inside clearly.

"Look," whispered Mike, pointing to the man and woman in the kitchen.

"There's your dad," Tanya whispered. Mike's father was alone in a storage room at the back of the restaurant. He was pacing, walking back and forth. He stopped and looked around. He seemed to be searching for a way out. Then he started pacing again.

"So those people are cooking while your father is in danger?" asked Mrs. Mendez. "I can't believe they would just stand there and cook at a time like this! Your poor father."

"What are they doing?" Tanya asked. The man and the woman were very busy stirring lots of bubbling pots. Mike pointed to a small bottle of purple liquid on the counter nearby. It looked a lot like the bottle of secret formula in Professor Perry's safe.

Mike, Tanya, and Mrs. Mendez tiptoed around to the back of the restaurant. They found an open door and quickly went inside.

Being able to look through walls really did save time. In a minute or two, they found the room where Professor Perry was being held. Mike unlocked the door easily.

"Mike! Tanya! Mrs. Mendez!" exclaimed Professor Perry. "I'm so glad to see you! How did you find me?"

"Well, that's a long story," said Mike. "What's going on, Dad?"

Professor Perry told them what had happened. Last week, he had come to this restaurant to meet someone from Smith Medical Company. The company was very interested in buying the secret formula to use in their mouthwash.

"You see," continued Professor Perry, "my formula tricks your taste buds. Whatever your put in your mouth tastes wonderful. Even really awful tasting stuff like cauliflower."

Mike and Tanya looked at each other. No wonder the carrotberries tasted so great after they'd been splashed by the secret formula!

"The owners of this restaurant must have overheard us talking," Professor Perry said.

"I get it!" said Mike. "They wanted to use the formula in their food."

"Exactly," said Professor Perry. "They could continue to make their tasteless food. But with my formula, everyone would think it was delicious. The Fowlers would get more customers and make more money."

"Those rude people at the lab own this restaurant?" asked Tanya.

"And they're the people who kidnapped you? They're the people who are cooking in the kitchen?" Mrs. Mendez asked.

"That's right," said the professor. "Mr. and Mrs. Fowler."

"Well, you can just tell them I'm never eating here!" huffed Mrs. Mendez.

The professor explained why the Fowlers had come to the lab that day. They had offered him a large amount of money for the formula. But the professor had said no. Before they left, Mr. Fowler grabbed a sample bottle of the formula off the lab counter.

"I must get that formula back," said Professor Perry. "It hasn't been properly tested. I have no idea what side effects it may have."

"I think we can help you with that, Dad," said Mike. He told him about the superpowers he and Tanya had gotten after eating the carrotberries.

"Oh, my," said the professor. "I wonder if the formula interacted with something in your carrotberries."

Professor Perry thought for awhile and then said, "I think I've got it. Carrots and strawberries are both rich in vitamin A. Vitamin A is very good for your eyes. The formula must have supercharged the vitamin A. So, the formula must affect more than just your taste buds."

"We have to get your sample back from these crooks," said Tanya.

"That's right," said Mike. "They can't get away with wrecking your lab and stealing your formula."

"Stealing?" said a voice behind them. "Oh, what a mean thing to say." The Fowlers suddenly walked into the room and slammed the door.

"You see, we're just borrowing the formula. We just want to see if it does what your father claims it can do," said Mrs. Fowler.

"That's right," Mr. Fowler said. "The professor will soon join us in the kitchen to add the formula to our food. If the formula works, the professor will sell it to us nicely. Or, we will get it another way. In the end, though, that formula will belong to us."

Quietly, Mike moved toward the door. He caught Tanya's eye.

Tanya understood what Mike wanted her to do. "It's great that you're interested in making things taste better." She talked fast, hoping to keep the Fowlers from noticing what Mike was doing.

Mike nodded. *Yea, Tanya! Keep talking!*

"We used the formula for our science fair project," Tanya went on. "Wow, did it make our foods taste better! I mean, a thousand times better! I bet you could serve cardboard dunked in that stuff and people would ask for more."

"What a great idea," said Mrs. Fowler.

Tanya kept talking about everything she could think of. She talked about how they wanted a food with carrot crunch and strawberry sweetness. She also talked about growing the vines. She talked as fast as she could.

All the time, Mike was moving slowly toward the door. He reached his hand out, hoping the Fowlers wouldn't take their eyes off Tanya.

Mr. Fowler tapped his foot impatiently. Tanya ignored him and went on. "And one day, the formula got splashed on our carrotberries by mistake. Then the most amazing thing happened—"

At that moment, Mike hit the light switch.

**1** Why do the Fowlers want Professor Perry's formula?

**2** How does the formula give Mike and Tanya special powers?

**3** Why does Mrs. Fowler like Tanya's idea for a menu item?

**4** What do you think will happen next?

# Sweet and Crunchy Success

"Hey! What's happening?"

"Who did that?"

"Turn those lights back on right now!"

The Fowlers stumbled around in the dark. "You won't get away with this!" shouted Mrs. Fowler.

"Quick!" yelled Mike. "Out!" He watched the Fowlers fall over each other as they searched for the light switch.

Thanks to the carrotberries, Mike and Tanya could see perfectly in the dark. In no time, they led Professor Perry and Mrs. Mendez out of the storage room. Tanya shut and locked the door.

Mike ran back to the kitchen and grabbed the stolen bottle of formula. Then everyone jumped back in Mrs. Mendez's car. She took off like a race car driver.

At the police station, Professor Perry explained everything that had happened. Well, almost everything. He didn't think they'd believe the carrotberry superpower part. Mike gave the officer Mrs. Fowler's tomato pin to use as evidence.

"I guess that's over," said Professor Perry as they left the police station. "Let's go back to The Plant and clean up."

Back at The Plant, Professor Perry said, "I'm glad the formula is safe from those two. Who knows what kinds of things they would have served as food."

"You mean like using grated pencil erasers instead of cheese?" Mike asked.

His father shuddered. "Anyway, I think we need a lot more work on that formula. It certainly had some strange effects on your carrotberries."

"Hey, Mike," Tanya exclaimed. "What are we going to do? The science fair is in two days and we've eaten most of our project!"

"Well, we still have a few carrotberries left on the vines," Mike said. "Dad, do you know how we can make them ripen really fast?"

"Well, actually I do," Professor Perry said. "You put them in a paper bag…"

"This doesn't involve another secret formula, does it?" asked Mike.

"No, it's just an old cook's trick," laughed his dad.

"Okay then," Mike said through a big yawn. He blinked hard. "Tanya, are you seeing spots?"

"Stripes," she answered. "I think the super-vision is wearing off."

Professor Perry cleared his throat. "Well, as I said, the formula needs a little work."

"Right," said Tanya and Mike together. *But let someone else test it,* they thought.

Two days later, the science fair judges were treated to a whole handful of ripe, delicious carrotberries. They all agreed that this was the best project they'd seen in a long time. And the tastiest!

Professor Perry and Mrs. Mendez waved happily as Mike and Tanya walked to the winner's platform. Mike had dreamed that the gold medal would look great around his neck. He was right. Tanya's medal looked great, too. The two smiled at each other. This was certainly one science fair project they would never forget!

UNDERSTANDING FICTION

1. How does Mike use a carrotberry superpower to help everyone escape?

2. What information does Professor Perry not tell the police?

3. Why don't Mike and Tanya want to use the secret formula again?

4. If you could have one superpower, what would it be? Explain your answer.